# CAT CRAZY

*Books in the Animal Ark Pets series*

1 Puppy Puzzle
2 Kitten Crowd
3 Rabbit Race
4 Hamster Hotel
5 Mouse Magic
6 Chick Challenge
7 Pony Parade
8 Guinea Pig Gang
9 Gerbil Genius
10 Duckling Diary
11 Lamb Lessons
12 Doggy Dare
13 Cat Crazy

# BEN M. BAGLIO

# CAT CRAZY

**Illustrated by
Paul Howard**

**Cover Illustration by
Chris Chapman**

A
**LITTLE APPLE**
PAPERBACK

SCHOLASTIC INC.
New York  Toronto  London  Auckland  Sydney
Mexico City  New Delhi  Hong Kong

To Billy, a very special kitten, much missed.


Special thanks to Narinder Dhami.

ISBN 0-439-05170-3

12 11 10 9 8 7 6 5 4 ‾ ‾                                        1 2 3 4 5/0

Printed in the U.S.A.                                                      40

First Scholastic Trade printing, October 2000

# *Contents*

1. A Picnic by the River    1
2. *Puss-in-Boats*    13
3. Mr. Pengelly    26
4. A Lost Cat    41
5. Looking for Queenie    53
6. Mandy's Idea    61
7. An Invitation    71
8. Helping Out    88
9. Open House    94
10. A Confession    106

# CAT CRAZY

# 1

# *A Picnic by the River*

"Mandy Hope, you want *another* cookie?" laughed Dr. Emily Hope, as Mandy opened the cookie tin. "You and James have both eaten enough to feed an army!"

Mandy grinned at her mother. "I was just wondering if there were any of those chocolate cookies left," she said.

"May I have one, too, please?" asked James eagerly. He was lying on the picnic blanket with his Labrador puppy, Blackie.

"There's only one." Mandy held up the cookie. "We'll share it."

Blackie woofed hopefully.

"Okay, Blackie." Mandy smiled at the puppy, who was wagging his tail like a little black flag. "We'll all share it!"

Dr. Adam Hope shook his head. "I've never seen two children and one dog eat so much in my life!" he said to his wife.

"I always seem to get hungrier on vacation!" said James with a grin. "And so does Blackie!"

The Hopes, Mandy's best friend, James Hunter, and, of course, Blackie, were on vacation for two weeks in the Gloucestershire countryside called the Cotswolds. Mandy and James hadn't been to the Cotswolds before, and they were enjoying walking and biking around the gently rolling hills and valleys. They weren't staying in one place but driving to a different Cotswold village every few days.

Yesterday they had arrived at their last stop, a small hotel in a village called Bilbury. Today was Wednesday. Mandy and James were determined to make the most of the last few days of the vacation before going home on Sunday morning.

"I think this is the best vacation I've ever had," Mandy said happily as she fed Blackie a tiny piece of cookie. "I'm so glad we came!"

"I'm really glad you asked Blackie and me to come, too," said James. "Blackie's been good, hasn't he?"

They all looked at Blackie, who was sitting very still and staring at the cookie Mandy was eating.

"He always is when there's food around!" Mandy laughed. She loved being on vacation with James and his dog. It was almost as good as having a pet of her own.

Mandy's parents were both vets and worked in a clinic built onto the back of their house in the village of Welford. Because the clinic was always so busy with other people's animals,

Mandy couldn't have a pet of her own. And it was difficult for Dr. Adam and Dr. Emily to take a vacation. But this time they'd managed to find another vet, Dr. Alison Morgan, to cover for them.

"Wouldn't it be great if we could have brought all the animals from Animal Ark on vacation with us?" said Mandy with a grin. "I wonder how they all are?"

Dr. Adam laughed. "I don't think there would have been room in the car for the rest of us!"

Dr. Emily put her arm around Mandy. "We'll call Dr. Morgan tonight and find out how everyone is doing," she promised.

James grinned. "Mandy doesn't forget about animals even on vacation."

"Of course I don't!" said Mandy. "And talking of animals, it's about time we took Blackie for a walk."

Blackie opened his eyes and pricked up his ears at the word *walk*.

James jumped up. "All right," he said, "but I've eaten so much, I can hardly move!"

"You'd better keep Blackie on his leash," said Dr. Adam. "We don't want him taking a swim in the river."

Mandy bent down and clipped the leash firmly to Blackie's collar. "We'd never get him out again!" she said. Although she and James had been trying to train Blackie for months, he still wouldn't always do as he was told. "Ready, James?"

James nodded.

"Don't be too long," Dr. Emily called after them as they set off along the riverbank.

"Look, James!" Mandy said, pointing at the water. "Aren't the dragonflies beautiful?"

They stopped for a few minutes to watch the dragonflies skimming over the surface of the river. But Blackie was soon tugging at the leash, so they walked on.

Mandy smiled. She loved having Blackie around, and James didn't mind sharing him at all. She bent down to pet the puppy, then handed the leash to James. "Here, it's your turn."

"Maybe we'd better go back now," said James, winding Blackie's leash firmly around his hand. "Your mom said not to go too far."

"Lazybones!" Mandy teased him. "We'll just go around the next bend of the river. Then we'll turn back."

James nodded. "Okay. But next time we have a picnic, remind me not to eat so much!"

They walked farther along the bank. The river twisted and turned in a long curve, and Mandy and James followed its path.

There were some ducks swimming in the water, and Blackie began to bark when he spotted them. The ducks swam off as fast as they could.

"He won't hurt you," James called. "He just wants to make friends, that's all." He turned to Mandy with a grin as the ducks flew off in all directions. "I don't think they believe me!"

But Mandy wasn't listening. She grabbed James's arm and pointed at something ahead of them. "Look, James!"

There was a small black cat sitting on the

riverbank. It was licking its leg with its pink tongue.

"Hello, kitty!" said James. The cat stopped washing and stared curiously at them.

"Isn't it gorgeous!" Mandy said. "Let's go and make friends."

"What about Blackie?" James asked, looking down at his puppy, who was sniffing around in the grass. "The cat might not like dogs."

Just then Blackie noticed the cat and pricked up his ears. He was used to cats, because James had one named Benji, but Blackie always got excited when he saw one. He started barking again. The black cat looked alarmed and jumped to its feet.

"Quiet, Blackie!" James gasped, trying to stop himself from being dragged along the riverbank. "You'll frighten it!"

Mandy frowned. "Look, James," she said in a worried voice. "I think the cat is hurt!"

James stared at the little black cat. He could see what Mandy meant. One of its front legs didn't look quite right. The cat was holding it

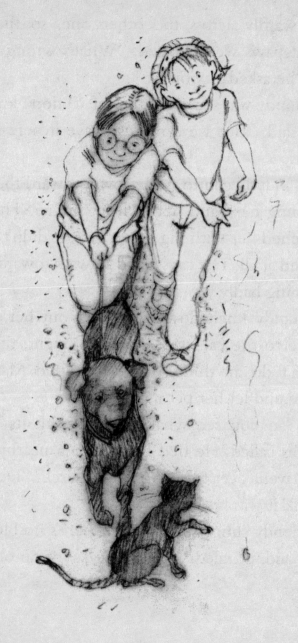

awkwardly across the other one, so that its front paws were crossed. "What's wrong with it?" he asked anxiously.

Mandy was staring at the cat. "I don't know," she said. "But we can't just leave it here if it's hurt."

Mandy began to walk slowly toward the cat, holding her hand out in front of her. The cat watched her with big green eyes. It didn't look scared at all. The cat started to walk toward her, limping badly.

Mandy knelt down and held out her hand close to the cat's face. For a moment, the cat didn't do anything. Then it sniffed Mandy's hand and let her pet its head.

"Can you see what's wrong with its leg?" James called. He tied Blackie to a nearby tree and went over to pet the cat himself. "Do you think it was hit by a car?"

Mandy shook her head. "There's no blood," she said, puzzled. "I think it may be an old injury."

"You mean it was hurt somehow and left with a limp?" James looked upset. "That's awful."

"I wonder where it's from," Mandy said, tickling the little cat's tummy. "Maybe it lives in the village."

Through the trees that grew along the riverbank they could just see the village where they were staying. It seemed a very long way for a little cat with a bad leg to walk.

Mandy looked worried. "I hope it isn't lost."

"Maybe we should take it back to your mom and dad," James suggested. Right at that moment, the little cat got up and started to limp away in the other direction.

"We'd better follow and make sure it's all right," Mandy decided quickly.

James went to get Blackie, and they all hurried after the little cat. The cat looked over its shoulder and saw them following but didn't seem to mind.

"We'd better not go too far," James said nervously. "Your mom and dad will be wondering where we are."

Mandy didn't answer. Instead she nudged James in the ribs and pointed down the river-bank.

"Wow!" she gasped. "Look at that!"

# 2

# Puss-in-Boats

"It's a boat full of cats!" said James, his eyes wide with amazement.

The boat was a long, thin barge, the kind of boat that people sometimes live in. It was painted red and blue, and there was a picture of a black-and-white cat painted on the side.

Above that, the name of the boat was written in red letters — *Puss-in-Boats.*

A coal-black cat, a marmalade cat, and a tabby cat were asleep on top of the cabin, all curled up together. Two black-and-white cats were eating from food bowls on the boat deck, and Mandy and James counted another six cats walking up and down or sitting, washing themselves. As they stared in amazement, the little black cat jumped gracefully from the riverbank onto the deck. Then it sat down to have another wash.

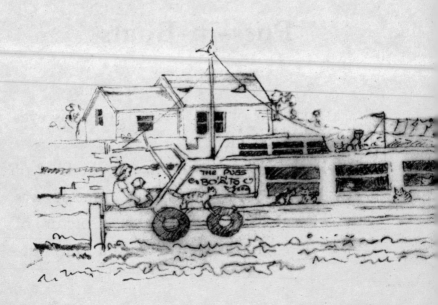

"*Puss-in-Boats,*" said James, with a grin. "I can see why it's called that!"

"Me, too!" Mandy agreed, her eyes shining. She'd never seen so many cats all together in one place. "Let's get closer."

Mandy, James, and Blackie hurried along the riverbank until they reached the barge. As they got closer, they could see that the boat was shabby and needed a coat of paint. But there were pots of flowers on the deck, and all the cats looked healthy and well fed.

"How many cats are there?" James asked in a dazed voice.

"Well, I can see eleven," said Mandy, as a big orange-and-white cat came in view from the other side of the boat. "No, twelve."

"Did you count the gray one near the flowers?" James asked, pointing it out.

Mandy couldn't remember, so they had to start counting all over again. Meanwhile, the little black cat was sniffing around the empty food bowls. When it realized there was no food left, it began to meow loudly.

"Who looks after all these cats?" James wondered.

Mandy was still counting under her breath. "Oh, no, now I've lost count again!" she sighed. "How many do you count, James?"

"Eighteen," said someone else's voice.

A blond boy about Mandy's age appeared from belowdecks and was smiling shyly at them. Mandy and James smiled back.

"Come on board and say hello to our cats,"

the boy said. "My mom won't mind, will you, Mom?"

A young woman in jeans who had the same color hair as the boy followed him onto the deck. She waved at Mandy and James. "Hello. I'm Lucy Browne, and this is my son, Martin. Do you like cats?"

"I'm Mandy Hope, and this is James Hunter," Mandy said, "and we love cats."

"Well, come and meet ours. We're always looking for volunteers to give them a cuddle." Lucy grinned at them. "It isn't easy finding the time to give eighteen cats all the love and attention they need!"

Mandy and James were thrilled. James tied Blackie to the nearest tree, and they stepped onto the barge. Blackie looked disappointed for a moment. Then he lay down, put his nose between his paws, and went to sleep.

As soon as Mandy and James were aboard, they were surrounded by cats. Mandy scooped up the nearest one into her arms, and it snuggled down on her shoulder. It was a big marmalade cat, and it had the loudest purr Mandy had ever heard.

"That's Pusskin," said Lucy. "He's our oldest cat. He's fifteen."

Mandy gave Pusskin a cuddle. He purred even louder and put his paws around her neck. Mandy didn't want to put him down, but there were so many other cats begging for attention that she had to. She knelt down and petted as many as she could, trying hard to remember all their names.

James was holding a beautiful tabby with big green eyes and an orange mark on her forehead. "What's this one called?" he asked.

"That's Penny," said Martin. "She catches anything that moves."

"And leaves it on the deck for us to trip over next morning!" added Lucy.

"Why do you have so many cats?" Mandy asked as she petted Lily, another black cat.

"Well, we had three cats of our own," Lucy began. "Then we took in a few strays, and

people started bringing us more and more," she explained. "Three of the cats were left homeless when their elderly owners died. I didn't have the heart to turn any of them away."

"Some of them have been badly treated," said Martin. He pointed to a very strange-looking cat that was asleep in a shady corner of the deck. "Like Muffin."

"Poor thing," said James. "He looks as if most of his fur has been shaved off."

"The vet had to do that," said Lucy. "Muffin's a Persian cat, and their fur has to be brushed regularly, or it gets all tangled up."

"You mean his owner didn't look after him properly?" Mandy asked. She hated it when people didn't take good care of their pets.

Lucy nodded. "Muffin's fur was such a mess, we couldn't brush it," she said. "But it'll grow back."

There was suddenly a loud *meow* behind them. They all jumped and turned around. The little black cat was still sitting by the empty food bowl.

Lucy laughed. "I think you've met Queenie, haven't you?"

"Yes." Mandy knelt down and petted her. "She's gorgeous! But what happened to her leg?"

"She got hit by a car," said Lucy, "and her owner didn't want her back, because her leg didn't heal properly."

"That's terrible!" said Mandy.

Queenie meowed again at the top of her voice, and Lucy covered her ears.

"She won't stop until we feed her," Lucy laughed.

"I'll feed her," Martin offered. "I think Effie needs feeding, too."

"Who's Effie?" James asked.

Lucy smiled. "She's the newest addition to our family — and she had four babies almost as soon as she arrived here!"

"Kittens!" said Mandy, her face lighting up. "Where are they?"

"Belowdecks," said Martin, pointing at the cabin door.

"All snuggled in a basket with their mom!" Lucy added. "They're only three weeks old."

"Where did Effie come from?" James asked.

"Mrs. Cox, who runs the village store, found her wandering around and brought her to us," Lucy explained. "She would have loved to keep the cat herself, but she's got a couple of dogs already."

"And we've taken in a couple of other cats from the village," Martin added. "Smokey was a stray that Mr. Tilbury brought to us, and Lily belonged to a family who moved away."

"May we see the kittens now?" Mandy asked eagerly.

"Of course, if you have time," said Lucy with a smile.

Mandy and James looked at each other, remembering they'd promised not to be away too long on their walk.

"My mom and dad will be waiting for us down the riverbank," Mandy said. She wanted to see the kittens, and there were still some cats she hadn't said hello to yet, but they couldn't keep her parents waiting much longer.

"Well, why don't you ask them if they'd like to come to *Puss-in-Boats* for a cup of tea?" suggested Lucy. "Then they can meet the cats and the kittens, too."

Mandy's eyes lit up. "That would be great!" she said. "Come on, James. Let's go and tell them."

Mandy and James stepped over the cats and climbed off the barge.

"We'll be back soon, we hope!" Mandy called, waving at their new friends. James untied Blackie, and the three of them ran back along the riverbank.

"There you are!" said Dr. Emily, as Mandy, James, and Blackie raced up to them. "We were beginning to wonder where you were."

"Oh, we've had a great time!" Mandy gasped. "We went on this barge, and we saw lots of cats!"

"Eighteen cats!" added James. "And Lucy

and Martin look after them, and they've invited us all for tea!"

Dr. Adam and Dr. Emily looked puzzled.

"Could one of you take a deep breath and go through that again?" asked Dr. Adam.

So Mandy told them the whole story.

"It sounds as if Lucy and her son are doing a very good job, looking after all those cats," said Dr. Emily. "We'd love to come and see them."

"Great!" Mandy jumped to her feet. "May we go right now?"

"Your mom and I had better pack up the picnic things first," said Dr. Adam, picking up the basket. "You go on ahead and tell Lucy and Martin that we're on our way."

"Okay!" Mandy and James were already off, running along the riverbank. Blackie was bounding along beside them.

"The boat's name is *Puss-in-Boats*," Mandy shouted over her shoulder. "You can't miss it!"

"No, I don't suppose there are many boats with eighteen cats!" Dr. Adam called back.

"Aren't Lucy and Martin great?" Mandy said

to James as they raced along the riverbank. "I don't know what would have happened to those cats if they weren't looking after them."

"I know," James replied. "How can people be so mean?"

"At least the cats are safe on *Puss-in-Boats* now," said Mandy.

They followed the bend in the river, and there was the barge, bobbing gently on the water.

"Look, there's Lucy," said James. "She's talking to someone."

Lucy was standing on the riverbank with a man and a woman. As Mandy and James got nearer, they could see that the man's face was red, as if he was angry about something.

"This isn't good enough, madam," they heard the man say in an angry voice. "As soon as I possibly can, I'm going to see to it that all of these cats are removed!"

# 3
# *Mr. Pengelly*

Mandy and James stood on the riverbank and looked at each other in shock. What was going on?

"Mr. Pengelly," Lucy was saying politely, "the cats really aren't doing any harm —"

"Well, I found one in my yard the other day, and the day before that!" Mr. Pengelly said an-

grily. He was a small, round man with gray hair and a gray beard. "It's not right keeping so many animals on a boat — it's a health hazard!"

"Why don't you come onto *Puss-in-Boats* and have a cup of tea?" Lucy suggested. "Then we can talk."

Mr. Pengelly shook his head. "I'm warning you," he said furiously. "No one in the village wants you here, and we're taking steps to make you move on! Come along, Marjorie."

Mr. Pengelly marched off, and the woman, who hadn't said a word, followed him. Lucy looked very upset, and so did Martin. James quickly tied up Blackie, while Mandy rushed up to Lucy.

"Who was that?" she asked.

Lucy sighed. "That's Mr. Pengelly and his wife," she said. "They live in the village, and he's been complaining about us ever since we arrived here, five weeks ago."

"Why?" James asked.

"He says the cats are a nuisance, and they go in his yard," Martin replied.

Lucy frowned. "I don't understand it," she said. "Most of the cats are so nervous, they never go as far as the village. They stay close to the boat."

"Doesn't he know you're looking after cats that have been badly treated?" Mandy asked. "Maybe if Mr. Pengelly knew that, he might calm down a little."

Lucy managed a smile. "He never gives me a chance. But I don't think it would make any difference."

"He wants us to move the boat somewhere else," added Martin. "But we can't, can we, Mom? The engine needs repairing."

Lucy nodded. "We barely managed to get it this far," she said. "If we're forced to go, we'll have to leave the boat behind and move into an apartment, and then, of course, we won't be able to take all the cats with us."

"There must be something we can do," Mandy said desperately. "Maybe we could help you find homes for them."

"We're always trying to find good homes,"

Martin said, bending down to pet Penny. "But most people don't want older cats."

"Well, let's have a snack, and we can talk about it later," Lucy said, smiling at Mandy and James. "Come onto the boat, and I'll fix something to eat."

Mandy and James looked at each other as they followed Lucy onto the barge. If only there was something that she and James could do to help, Mandy thought. But what?

As before, Mandy and James were surrounded by cats as soon as they stepped aboard the boat. But this time Mandy noticed how many other cats *didn't* come out to be petted. Some stayed back, hiding themselves away and looking fearfully at Mandy and James. Mandy guessed that these were the animals who had been treated so badly. They were scared of humans they didn't know. What would happen to these cats if Lucy and Martin had to leave *Puss-in-Boats*?

"There's your mom and dad, Mandy," said

James. In the distance they could see Dr. Adam and Dr. Emily walking along the riverbank, carrying the picnic basket.

Mandy turned to Lucy and Martin. "My mom and dad are both vets," she said. "I could ask if they would check over all the cats for you, if you like. If the cats are healthy, then maybe Mr. Pengelly won't have so much to complain about."

Lucy's face lit up. "That would be wonderful," she said. "At the moment I have to take the cats to a free clinic, and it's miles away from here."

The Hopes were getting closer now, so Mandy and James scrambled off the boat and ran to meet them.

"Dad!" Mandy gasped, "There's this mean man called Mr. Pen something —"

"Pengelly," said James.

"And he's trying to get rid of *Puss-in-Boats*!" Mandy continued breathlessly. "And Lucy and Martin might have to move into an apartment —"

"And they won't be able to take the cats with them," James finished off.

Dr. Adam held up his hand. "Hold on a minute, you two! Let's say hello to your new friends before you tell us exactly what's going on."

"Come on, Dad!" said Mandy eagerly. She grabbed her father's hand and started tugging him toward the barge, where Lucy and Martin were waving at them.

"Maybe Lucy and Martin would like us to give the cats a quick checkup while we're here," Dr. Emily suggested as they walked up to the boat. "It can't be easy looking after so many cats."

"Oh, thanks, Mom!" said Mandy. "I hoped you'd say that!"

Lucy and Martin were waiting for them on the deck.

"Hello," said Lucy. "Welcome to *Puss-in-Boats*!"

"Hello," Dr. Emily smiled as she looked around. "What a wonderful name for a boat full of cats!"

Lucy and Martin looked pleased. For the next few minutes, everyone was busy talking and petting all the cats that curled around their ankles and jumped up onto their laps.

"Would you like to look around the boat before we have something to eat?" Lucy asked.

Mandy's eyes lit up. At last she was going to see the kittens!

*Puss-in-Boats* wasn't very big, but everything was neat and tidy. Lucy and Martin took their visitors around the deck and then to the rooms below. The two bedrooms, kitchen, and bathroom were narrow and cramped, but everything was clean.

"Oh, who painted these?" said Mandy. She'd just spotted some watercolor paintings of cats pinned to the cabin walls.

"I did," said Lucy. "I sell them to raise money to look after us and the cats."

"They're beautiful!" said Mandy. She pointed to one of the paintings. "That's Pusskin, isn't it?"

"And that's Queenie!" said James. Lucy had

painted Queenie, the little black cat with the limp, sitting with her injured leg crossed over the other. She looked just like she had when Mandy and James first saw her.

The kittens and their mother were in a basket under a low, narrow table. Mandy waited impatiently as Lucy knelt down and gently pulled the basket into view. Five sleepy faces looked up at them. Effie, the mother, was black and white, and so were the kittens, although their markings were all different.

"Oh, they're gorgeous!" Mandy said softly.

Lucy had warned them that Effie was a nervous cat, so they all stayed still and quiet as she lifted the kittens gently out of the basket. She put the biggest one into Mandy's arms.

"This one's called Button," she said. "The others are Candy, Snoopy, and Joe."

Even though Button was the biggest of the four, he was still tiny. He was black all over except for his white socks. Button looked up at Mandy and meowed.

"He's adorable!" Mandy said happily, rubbing her cheek against the kitten's soft fur.

They played with the kittens for a while, and then they all went back on deck and had tea and cookies. As they were finishing tea, Dr. Adam turned to Lucy. "Mandy and James were saying you've been having problems with someone from the village?"

Lucy quickly explained about Mr. Pengelly. "We've only been here a little while," she said. "But he hasn't been happy since we've arrived."

Dr. Adam frowned. "I think Mr. Pengelly's being a little unfair," he said. He put out his hand and scooped up the cat nearest to him. "Let's start checking the cats. I think I recognize this one from Lucy's picture!"

"That's Queenie," said Mandy. "She's the one who brought us here!"

Dr. Adam gave Queenie a quick checkup. "Well, you'll be glad to know that, apart from her leg, she seems to be very healthy. Now, who's next?"

Everyone helped to bring the cats to the vets to be checked. But some of the cats didn't want to be picked up.

"Come out, Smokey!" gasped Martin. Some of the cats had gone belowdecks to hide. Martin was trying to coax Smokey out from under one of the beds. "No one's going to hurt you."

Mandy came down from the deck to see what was going on. "I don't think she believes you!" she said. "Maybe you could get her out with some food?"

"Good idea," said Martin. "She loves cheese. I'll go and get some."

Martin managed to get Smokey out with a small piece of cheese. Almost all the cats had been checked by now. Apart from Pusskin, whose sore eye Lucy had already noticed, the cats seemed to be in the best of health.

"Is that all of them?" Mandy asked. There were so many cats, it was impossible for her to keep count.

Lucy frowned. "I think there's just Jessie left.

She's another of our nervous ones, and she's probably hidden herself away."

"What does she look like?" Mandy asked.

"She's black and white." Lucy smiled. "And she's easy to recognize, because she's much too fat!"

Mandy wandered around the deck, keeping a sharp lookout for Jessie. Then she spotted her. The small, round cat had wedged herself into a tiny gap between two life belts.

"Come on, Jessie," Mandy murmured gently. She knelt down and held out her hand. To her amazement, Jessie put out her paw and slapped Mandy's hand away.

Mandy jumped. She wasn't hurt, because Jessie hadn't put her claws out. Mandy was just surprised. She put out her hand again, and again the cat slapped it away.

Lucy saw what was happening and came over. "Jessie used to belong to a family who teased her all the time," Lucy said quietly, as she knelt down by Mandy. "And now, if

Jessie's scared, she hits out at people with her paw."

Mandy felt very upset. The cat looked so unhappy. "Will she come out for you?" Mandy asked.

"She might," Lucy replied. Then Lucy knelt down, and after a few minutes she managed to get Jessie out for a checkup.

"Pusskin's eye infection should clear up in a couple of days, if you bathe it," said Dr. Adam as he put his jacket back on. "It isn't serious."

"Thank you so much," said Lucy gratefully. "I was going to take him to the free clinic tomorrow, so you've saved me a trip."

"How long are you staying in the village?" Martin asked, as the Hopes and James got ready to leave.

"Until Sunday," said Dr. Emily. She looked at Mandy and James, who were saying good-bye to all the cats. "So I don't think you've seen the last of us!"

"Oh, please come and see us whenever you

like!" said Lucy. "What about tomorrow morning?"

"We'd love to!" said Mandy eagerly.

They left the boat, waving to Lucy and Martin and the cats, and began the walk back to the village.

Mandy could not stop thinking about Jessie and Smokey, who were so scared and unhappy. She turned to James. "We can't let Mr. Pengelly force Lucy and Martin to abandon *Puss-in-Boats*!"

"That's just what I was thinking!" James said. "But what can we do?"

"I don't know yet," said Mandy. Then she added, in her most determined voice, "But we'll have to think of something!"

# 4

# *A Lost Cat*

Thursday morning was bright and sunny. Mandy and James were up early. Since it wasn't time for breakfast yet, they took Blackie out into the garden behind the hotel.

"I dreamed about cats all night!" James said with a grin.

"So did I!" said Mandy. "I can't wait to go back to *Puss-in-Boats* today."

"Me, too," James agreed. Then he frowned. "I hope Mr. Pengelly doesn't come by, though."

Mandy sighed. "I just wish he would give Lucy and Martin a chance," she said. "What is going to happen to all the cats, if they have to leave the boat?"

James looked worried. "Have you come up with any ideas about how we can help them?"

Mandy shook her head. "Not really," she answered, and then she smiled. "But remember Tibby's six kittens? We found good homes for them, didn't we?"

James nodded, looking more cheerful. "Yes, we did!" Then his face fell again. "That was back home in Welford, though. It's different here. We don't know anybody."

Mandy knew what James meant. They couldn't just walk up to people they didn't know and ask them if they wanted a cat. And as Martin had said yesterday, older cats were more difficult to find homes for. "We'll just have to do our very best," she said firmly.

"Yes, we will," James agreed, looking around. "Oh, no! Blackie! Stop that!" he shouted.

Blackie was having a good time digging a hole in one of the flower beds and sending earth flying everywhere. James raced over and dragged the puppy out.

"Bad dog, Blackie!" he said, pointing sternly at the Labrador. Blackie just wagged his tail and jumped up to lick James's hand.

"Good morning, you two." Mrs. Ross, the owner of the hotel, opened the door and came out into the garden. She was a round woman with graying hair and a warm smile. As soon as Blackie saw Mrs. Ross, he pulled away from James and bounded up to her, wagging his tail. "And how's Blackie this morning?"

"Just as naughty as usual," said James. "I'm sorry, Mrs. Ross, but he's dug a hole in one of your flower beds."

"Oh, don't worry about that," said Mrs. Ross

with a smile, as she bent down to pet the excited young dog. "It doesn't look like there's any serious damage. Are you ready for breakfast?"

"Yes, please," James said eagerly.

"Well, why don't I give Blackie his breakfast, while you two go and wash your hands?" Mrs. Ross suggested, with a twinkle in her eyes. "I'm sure he's hungry after all that digging!"

"Thanks, Mrs. Ross," James said gratefully, as she took Blackie indoors to the kitchen.

Mandy looked thoughtful as they washed their hands. "I wonder what Mrs. Ross thinks about *Puss-in-Boats*," she said, as she reached for the soap. "Mr. Pengelly said that no one in the village wants the barge here. But perhaps some people don't feel like that. Mrs. Cox, for instance — she asked Lucy to take in Effie, didn't she?"

"Yes," said James. "I bet Mrs. Ross doesn't mind *Puss-in-Boats*. She loves animals."

"There aren't many hotels that let you bring

your pet on vacation with you," Mandy agreed.

James grinned. "Especially pets like Blackie!"

The Hopes were already sitting at the breakfast table in the dining room when Mandy and James hurried in.

"Hello, you two," Dr. Emily said, smiling at them. "Do you want cereal?"

"Yes, please," Mandy said. "We're starving!"

"What a surprise!" laughed Dr. Adam, passing James the box of cornflakes. "So, I expect you two would like to go back to *Puss-in-Boats* this morning, wouldn't you?"

Mandy nodded eagerly. "Lucy said we could."

"All right," Dr. Emily said, with a smile. "We'll take you there after we've finished breakfast. Your dad and I have decided to go for a long walk this morning."

Mrs. Ross came in just then, carrying a large tray loaded with tea and toast. She brought it over to their table.

"Here you go." She beamed at them. "There's scrambled eggs, bacon, and sausages coming in just a moment, and I've fed Blackie, too. Goodness me, James, that dog of yours can eat!"

James grinned. "I know," he said. "Eating and misbehaving are Blackie's two favorite things!"

"What are you all planning to do today?" Mrs. Ross asked as she set out the teacups.

"James and I are going to *Puss-in-Boats* to see Lucy and Martin and their cats," said Mandy. "Do you know them, Mrs. Ross?"

"Yes, I do." Suddenly Mrs. Ross looked sad. "Lucy and Martin helped me to look for my cat when he didn't come home a few weeks ago. I don't know what I'd have done without them."

"I didn't know you had a cat, Mrs. Ross," Mandy said.

"Poor William was too ill to make it home on his own," Mrs. Ross sighed, looking even more upset. "He died a few days later. He was sixteen years old, so he'd had a good life. I miss him, though."

Mandy bit her lip. "I'm sorry, Mrs. Ross."

Mrs. Ross smiled at her a bit tearfully and then began to bustle around the table, pouring out the tea. "Well, anyway, Lucy and Martin seem very nice."

"They are," said James.

"They're doing a good job of looking after all those cats, too," remarked Dr. Adam. "But we've heard that some people in the village aren't happy about them being here."

Mrs. Ross frowned. "That's true," she said. "Some villagers think that the cats are a nuisance and that the boat's too small to have so many cats on it."

"It's very clean, though," Mandy pointed out, "and so are the cats."

Mrs. Ross nodded. "Some people are worried that Mrs. Browne might take in more and more strays. I suppose they're concerned that the village might be overrun with cats." She finished pouring out the tea. "Still, Lucy was very helpful to me. And I know for a fact that she looked after Miss Dawson's cat when she had to go into hospital for a few days."

Mandy was pleased. It looked like there were several people who wouldn't support Mr. Pengelly. She wondered if Mrs. Ross had heard about his threat to get rid of *Puss-in-Boats.*

"Do you know Mr. Pengelly, Mrs. Ross?" she asked.

"Oh, yes, dear." Mrs. Ross frowned. "I've heard he's not at all happy about *Puss-in-Boats.*"

"No, he isn't," said James. "We saw him there yesterday."

Mrs. Ross shook her head. "I wouldn't worry about Harry Pengelly," she said. "He's not a bad person, but he's always upset about something. Now I'd better get back to my kitchen, or there'll be no scrambled eggs for you today!"

Mandy frowned as Mrs. Ross went out. In spite of what the hotel owner had said, she was still worried. Mrs. Ross might not take any notice of Mr. Pengelly, but other people in the village might.

After breakfast, the Hopes and James walked over to *Puss-in-Boats*. While Mandy and James visited Lucy and Martin, Dr. Adam and Dr. Emily were going to take Blackie with them on their country walk. The sun was getting warmer now, and there wasn't a cloud in the deep blue sky.

Mandy and James ran eagerly on ahead, along the riverbank, with Blackie running beside them. They raced around the bend in the river. Lucy was standing on the deck of *Puss-in-Boats*. They waved at her.

"We'll say a quick hello, and then we'll be off," said Dr. Adam as he and Dr. Emily caught up.

They all went over to the barge. Lucy was still on deck, but Mandy couldn't see Martin anywhere.

"Hello, Lucy," called Dr. Emily.

Lucy hurried across the deck of the barge toward them. "Hello, how nice to see you all again."

"We're off on a walk," said Dr. Adam. "We'll be back for Mandy and James in a couple of hours, if that's all right?"

"That's fine," said Lucy.

Mandy and James climbed onto *Puss-in-Boats*.

"'Bye then, you two," called Dr. Emily as she, Dr. Adam, and Blackie turned to leave. "Be good!"

"We will!" Mandy called back.

"Mom?" Martin suddenly appeared from below deck. He looked worried. "I can't find her. She isn't in the cabin." Then he saw Mandy and James. "Oh, hi!"

"Hello, Martin." Mandy looked puzzled. "Have you lost one of the cats?"

"It's Queenie," Martin said miserably. "We've looked all over the boat, and she isn't here."

"We haven't seen her since last night," Lucy

added, looking worried. "She's never been gone this long before."

"We'll help you look for her. Right, Mandy?" James said.

"Of course we will," Mandy said. She couldn't bear to think of the little cat with the injured leg lost somewhere, cold, and hungry. "Let's start right away!"

# 5

# *Looking for Queenie*

"Maybe we should look for Queenie along the riverbank," Mandy suggested. "That's where James and I first saw her."

"Good idea," said Lucy. "If you, Martin, and James go one way, I'll go the other."

They all climbed off the barge and onto the riverbank.

"Don't go too far," Lucy called after them.

Mandy, Martin, and James walked slowly along, calling Queenie's name. They searched the bushes along the riverbank but couldn't find Queenie anywhere. They went on until they had followed the path around the bend in the river.

"I think we'd better go back," Martin said.

Mandy stared along the riverbank. There was no sign of the little black cat anywhere. "Where can Queenie be?" Mandy asked miserably, as they started back toward the boat.

"You don't think she might have fallen in the river, do you?" asked James.

Martin shook his head. "Queenie hates the water. She won't go anywhere near it."

"All cats are like that, aren't they?" said James.

Martin smiled. "Not all of them," he said. "We used to have a cat named Victor who loved swimming!"

Mandy thought hard for a minute. "Do you

think Queenie might have gone to the village?" she suggested.

"Maybe," Martin said. "Let's see if Mom has had any luck."

They got back to *Puss-in-Boats* just a few minutes before Lucy came hurrying toward them from the opposite direction. Mandy, James, and Martin were waiting eagerly for her, but then they saw that she was alone.

"Mandy suggested we try looking in the village, Mom," said Martin.

Lucy nodded. "That's a good idea. Let's go."

Lucy and Martin knew a footpath that cut across the fields and was much quicker than going by road.

The village was small and very pretty, with its old stone church and winding streets full of thatched cottages. They stopped by the churchyard, and Lucy turned to the others. "I think we'd better split up again," she said. "I'll go this way." She pointed down the hill. "You three can look around the houses behind the church."

Mandy, James, and Martin nodded.

"I'll meet you back here in ten minutes," Lucy called over her shoulder as she set off. "Don't be late!"

"Maybe we ought to look for Queenie in the churchyard, too," Mandy suggested. "There are lots of places she could be hiding."

But Queenie wasn't in the churchyard.

Behind the church was a row of thatched cottages. All of the cottages had large front yards filled with brightly colored flowers and shrubs. Mandy, James, and Martin began to walk along the road, staring into all the yards.

"I've just remembered who lives in one of these cottages," Martin said suddenly.

"Who?" asked James.

"Mr. Pengelly!" Martin looked worried. "I hope Queenie isn't in his yard!"

Mandy frowned. "So do I!"

"Mr. Pengelly said he'd found a cat from *Puss-in-Boats* in his yard," James remembered. "But he didn't say which one."

"Which house is Mr. Pengelly's, Martin?" Mandy asked anxiously.

Martin pointed to the next house in the row. "Number 8."

They stopped outside the gate and glanced quickly around the front yard. Mandy felt very nervous.

"I don't think Queenie's here," Martin said, sounding relieved.

"No," Mandy said. "Thank goodness!"

"Just a minute," James said suddenly. "Something just moved — over there in the flower bed!"

Martin and Mandy looked where James was pointing, and Mandy's heart sank. There was Queenie, sitting under a large shrub, washing herself. After a few seconds, she started to settle down, looking as if she'd found the perfect spot for a nap.

"We've got to get her out," Mandy said desperately, "before Mr. Pengelly sees her!"

"Queenie!" Martin called softly.

Queenie opened her big green eyes and peered out through the leaves. She saw Martin and meowed a greeting. Then she yawned and closed her eyes again.

"Queenie!" Martin whispered again, but the cat paid no attention.

"She's too sleepy to move," Mandy said. "We'll have to go and get her ourselves!"

Martin was already unlatching the gate. "I'll be as quick as I can," he whispered. "Let's hope no one sees us!"

He hurried into Mr. Pengelly's yard, dashed over to the flower bed, and scooped Queenie up into his arms. Queenie was surprised, but then she snuggled down on Martin's shoulder and began to purr.

"Now get out of there!" Mandy said breathlessly.

Just then they heard the sound of a door

opening. With sinking hearts, Mandy, James, and Martin looked toward the house.

Mr. Pengelly was standing on his door-step with a shopping bag in his hand, staring in amazement. "What are you doing in my yard?"

# 6

# *Mandy's Idea*

For a moment, the three of them were too shocked to say anything. Then Mandy stepped forward. "We're very sorry, Mr. Pengelly," she said in a shaky voice. "We didn't mean any harm. Martin had to get his cat back, that's all."

Mr. Pengelly looked at Queenie and frowned. "That cat is always coming into my

61

yard!" he said angrily. "I've had enough of this!"

"What on earth is going on?"

Everyone looked around. Lucy was hurrying toward them, looking worried.

"Mom!" Martin rushed over and put Queenie into her arms. "We found Queenie in Mr. Pengelly's yard."

"Yes, and I came out and found your son in here without my permission!" snapped Mr. Pengelly.

"Oh, dear!" said Lucy.

"Sorry, Mr. Pengelly," said Martin.

The old man frowned. "This is just what I've been complaining about, Mrs. Browne!" he snapped. "That cat keeps coming into my yard and digging up my flower beds."

"She wasn't doing any harm," Martin argued. "She was just asleep."

Mr. Pengelly looked even more annoyed. "That's all very well, but what if she starts encouraging your other cats to come and sleep in my yard? I will not have it!"

Suddenly, Mandy got a picture in her mind of Queenie leading all the other cats from *Puss-in-Boats* in a long line into Mr. Pengelly's yard. It was such a funny thought that she wanted to laugh, but she didn't dare, he looked so angry.

"I can't understand why Queenie would come into your yard and no one else's," Lucy was saying. "No one else has complained."

"Well, what are you going to do about it?" Mr. Pengelly folded his arms and glared at them.

"We'll keep an eye on Queenie and try to make sure she doesn't go far from the boat," Lucy promised.

Mandy frowned. That wouldn't be easy. It was practically impossible to keep cats in one place, without locking them up.

Mr. Pengelly shook his head. "I'm afraid that's not good enough, Mrs. Browne. I've decided to start a petition to make you and your boat move away from here. I'm going to get everyone in the village to sign it!"

"A petition!" Mandy gasped. She looked at Martin and James. Things were going from bad to worse.

"Please, Mr. Pengelly," said Lucy, "can't we talk about this?"

"There's nothing to talk about," said the old man, and he marched off down the street.

"What a mean man!" said James.

Lucy sighed. "I don't think he's being very fair," she said, "but Queenie *was* in his yard."

"How many people do you think will sign the petition, Lucy?" Mandy asked anxiously.

"I don't know," Lucy replied. "I haven't had any other complaints, so maybe he won't get many." But she didn't sound too sure.

"Mrs. Ross won't sign it," said James.

"No, I'm sure she won't," Mandy agreed. But she was very worried about how many other people in the village would.

Lucy managed a smile. "Well, that's one person on our side, anyway! Come on, let's go back to *Puss-in-Boats*."

They set off for the barge.

"Do you want me to carry Queenie for a while?" Mandy asked Lucy. "Your arms must be tired."

"Thanks, Mandy," Lucy replied gratefully. She gave Queenie to Mandy, and the little black cat settled herself down on Mandy's shoulder. She seemed to be enjoying the ride.

As she walked along, stroking Queenie's warm fur, Mandy thought about what she and James could do to help Lucy and Martin and the cats. They couldn't just let Mr. Pengelly go

ahead with his petition and force *Puss-in-Boats* to leave or close down. They had to fight back. But how?

"Mandy?"

Mandy was thinking so hard that she didn't realize that James was speaking to her. Then she blinked. "Sorry, James. What did you say?"

"Queenie's gone to sleep on your shoulder!" James grinned at her. "She must be tired out after all that excitement!"

Mandy gently hugged the little cat, and Queenie started to purr sleepily. "I was just thinking about Mr. Pengelly," Mandy said. "If he's going to start a petition, then we have to do something, too."

"But what?" asked Martin.

Mandy frowned. "If everyone in the village knew what a good job *Puss-in-Boats* is doing, they wouldn't sign the petition."

"Do people in the village know about the cats?" James asked Lucy and Martin as they walked along the riverbank.

Lucy shrugged. "Well, I suppose some of them do," she said. "I've helped a few people out when their cats needed looking after, but we don't know that many people in the village."

James looked at Martin. "Haven't you made any friends here yet?"

Martin shook his head. "We got here too late for me to start at the village school last term," he said. "I was going to go there after this vacation. But now it doesn't look like we'll be here . . ." His voice trailed away.

They were close to *Puss-in-Boats* now. Penny and Pusskin, who were sitting on the riverbank, saw them and came to meet them.

James knelt down to pet the two cats. "It's too bad," he sighed. "If only everyone in the village could come and see the cats and get to know them, I'm sure they wouldn't sign Mr. Pengelly's petition."

Mandy gasped, and her face lit up. "James," she said softly, "you're a genius!"

James looked puzzled. "I am?" he said, pushing his glasses up his nose.

"Lucy," Mandy said, her voice trembling with excitement, "What about having an open house?"

"An open house?" Lucy repeated.

"Yes, so that everyone in the village can come and visit *Puss-in-Boats!*" Mandy explained breathlessly. "Then they can meet the cats and see how well you look after them!"

"Oh, Mandy, what a great idea!" said Lucy, a huge smile spreading across her face.

Mandy turned red. "Well, it was James's idea really," she pointed out.

"No, the open house was your idea, and I think it's great!" said James enthusiastically.

"So do I," Martin added.

Mandy looked pleased. "We can make some posters to advertise it," she said, "and put them up around the village. We want everyone to come."

"Even Mr. and Mrs. Pengelly?" asked James.

"*Especially* them!" Mandy said firmly. "And

we could put out deck chairs and tables and sell refreshments. What do you think, Lucy?"

Lucy nodded. "It's a good idea. We can't have too many people on the barge at one time, though. There isn't room, and it wouldn't be safe."

"We could put the table and chairs on the riverbank, next to the barge," James suggested. "And we could decorate the boat with balloons and streamers."

"That would be lovely," Lucy agreed. "And I could bake a few cakes and cookies to sell."

"And we could sell cups of tea and coffee and lemonade," James said eagerly.

"Maybe you could sell some of your paintings as well, Mom," Martin suggested.

"Why not?" Lucy agreed, as they all climbed aboard the barge. "We might even make some money for repairs!"

"Oh, I hope so!" said Mandy. Then, even if Lucy and Martin had to move, at least they wouldn't have to give up the boat and leave the cats behind.

"When shall we hold the open house?" asked Martin.

Lucy thought for a minute. "We'll have it on Saturday afternoon, the day before Mandy and James leave."

"But will we have enough time to get everything ready?" Mandy asked anxiously.

"Of course we will!" said Lucy. "Anyway, we can't have the open house without you two. After all, it was your idea!" She put her arm around Mandy's shoulder, which woke Queenie up. She opened her eyes and meowed grumpily.

"Don't worry, Queenie!" laughed Mandy. "You can be the star of the open house!"

"We'd better get started on some posters right away," said Lucy. "We must let everyone in the village know about the open house, and we don't have much time."

Mandy nodded. She was determined to make the event a big success. *Puss-in-Boats* was depending on them.

# 7

# *An Invitation*

Mandy, James, and Martin were sitting on the grassy riverbank with paper and paints spread out all around them.

"How are you doing?" called Lucy. She was sitting on the deck of the barge making a list of all the things they needed for Saturday afternoon.

Mandy held up her poster for Lucy to see. "Open House at *Puss-in-Boats*!" it read in large, colorful letters. She had drawn a black cat underneath the words. "That's supposed to be Queenie," she said, frowning at her drawing, "but I don't think it looks much like her!"

James and Martin were also hard at work. James's poster read:

Are you CAT CRAZY?
Then why not come to the Open House
at *Puss-in-Boats*?
This Saturday at 2 o'clock.

"I think I'll draw a picture of the barge at the bottom," James decided.

Martin had written the same words as James in the middle of his poster, and now he was drawing a border of cats around the edge of the paper.

"Make sure the posters are really bold and bright!" Lucy called from the barge. "We've got to make people notice them!"

"Hello, everyone!"

They all looked up. Dr. Adam and Dr. Emily and Blackie were walking along the riverbank toward them.

"Mom! Dad!" Mandy jumped to her feet and raced to meet them. James and Martin followed her. Blackie saw them and began to bark joyfully.

"Did you have a good walk?" James asked as Blackie hurled himself into his arms.

"Yes, thank you, James," said Dr. Adam.

"And what have you three been up to?" asked Dr. Emily curiously. She could see that Mandy, James, and Martin were all nearly bursting with excitement.

Mandy explained about the open house.

"What a good idea!" said Dr. Emily. "We'll help, won't we, Adam?"

"Of course," said Dr. Adam with a smile. "Just tell us what you want us to do."

"Thank you," said Lucy gratefully as she climbed off the boat to join them. "But we don't want to spoil your vacation. And, anyway, there isn't much to do until Saturday."

"We're all going out tomorrow," said Dr. Emily.

Mandy suddenly remembered that the next day they were going to visit an old friend of her father's, Roger Thomas, who ran a wildlife hospital not far from Bilbury. She had really been looking forward to it, but with the excitement of the open house, she had forgotten all about it. Still, as Lucy had said, once the posters were up, there wasn't much more they could do until Saturday.

Lucy invited Dr. Emily and Dr. Adam onto the barge for a cup of tea, but they wanted to get back to their room to change their clothes.

"I can drop Mandy and James off when we've finished putting up the posters, if you like," Lucy suggested.

"Thank you," Dr. Emily said. "That would save us a trip back here."

"We'll see you all in an hour or two, then,"

called Dr. Adam as he and Dr. Emily walked along the riverbank with Blackie.

Mandy, James, and Martin continued making their posters, while Lucy went back to her list.

Mandy finished first. She rolled the poster up carefully and put it with the others they had already made. They would have six posters to put up around the village. Soon everyone would know about the open house.

Mandy wondered nervously how many villagers would actually come. Mr. Pengelly wouldn't, she thought, her heart sinking. But Mrs. Ross had said that Mr. Pengelly wasn't a bad person. Maybe he would give *Puss-in-Boats* another chance if they could just make him see how important it was.

Mandy had an idea. She picked up a piece of paper, folded it in two to make a card, and began to draw on the front of it.

"What are you doing?" asked Martin.

"Just wait and see," Mandy said mysteriously.

James and Martin looked at each other. "I

think she's up to something," said James. "Mandy always has a plan."

When the posters were finished, they walked to the village to put them up. They stopped near the churchyard gate. Just to the side of the gate there was a large bulletin board with a couple of posters, one about a village square dance and another giving the times of the church services.

"I'll ask the priest if I can put one here," Lucy decided, taking three posters from Martin. "And one could go outside the school and another outside the village hall."

"We could put one on the community board on the green," Martin suggested. "Lots of people would see it there."

"And we could ask Mrs. Ross to put one in the window of the hotel," James added.

"Good idea," said Lucy. "Then we'll only have one left. Where can we put it?"

"I know!" Mandy said suddenly. "What about the store? I'm sure Mrs. Cox wouldn't mind. After all, Lucy helped her by taking Effie and her kittens in."

"That's a great idea!" said Martin. "Lots of people go to the store every day."

Lucy went to find the priest. Meanwhile, Mandy, James, and Martin walked to the village green and stopped at the community board. There wasn't anything on it except a poster about a mother-and-baby group at the church hall. Carefully Martin unrolled one of their posters and pinned it in the middle of the board. They all stood back to admire it.

"Now the store," said Martin. "It's just across the village green."

James and Martin set off across the grass, but the lace on one of Mandy's shoes had come undone, so she knelt down to retie it. As she did so, two women carrying shopping baskets stopped by the board.

"Look at that, Betty," said one of them, a short woman with dark hair. "There's an open house on Saturday on that boat — the one with all the cats."

"You know I can't stand cats, Vera," said her friend. She was taller than the first woman and wore large horn–rimmed glasses. "Nasty, dirty creatures they are."

Mandy's heart sank as she tied her shoelace. She hoped there weren't too many other people in the village who shared this view.

"I found my garbage can lid knocked off again this morning, and there was trash all over my garden walk," Betty went on. "I bet it was those dirty cats."

"It could have been a fox, Betty," Vera pointed out quickly. "I like cats myself, you know. We used to have a lovely tabby named George."

"I hear Harry Pengelly's starting up a petition to make that boat move," Betty remarked. "I think I'll sign it."

"Oh, but I don't think they're doing any harm," Vera argued. "I might drop in on this open house, just to see what's going on."

Mandy ran to catch up with James and Martin. She couldn't help worrying about how many people in the village would agree with Mr. Pengelly and Betty about the cats. They wouldn't know for sure, though, until the afternoon of the open house. It all depended on how many people turned up. Betty's friend didn't sound too sure about whether she was going to come. What if no one came?

Mandy decided not to tell James and Martin what the two women had said. There was no point in them all worrying.

"Let's go in and see Mrs. Cox," said Martin.

They were about to go into the store when the door opened, and Mrs. Ross came out.

"Hello, Mrs. Ross," James said. "We were coming to see you later!"

Mrs. Ross looked puzzled. "What for?" she asked curiously.

Quickly Mandy explained about the open house. "And we were wondering if you would put up a poster in the window of the hotel," she finished.

Mrs. Ross beamed at them. "What a wonderful idea!" she said. "Of course I'll put a poster up! But I hope you'll let me help out a little more than that."

"Yes, please!" said Mandy eagerly.

"Well, for one thing, I have lots of deck chairs and garden tables you can borrow." Mrs. Ross smiled at them. "I keep them for my guests, so I have more than most people."

"Thanks, Mrs. Ross!" said James.

"And I could do some baking for the refreshments table," Mrs. Ross added. "How about that?"

"That would be wonderful," said Martin gratefully.

"It's the least I can do after you and your mom helped me find William," said Mrs. Ross. She took one of the posters and hurried off down the road.

"Isn't she nice?" said Mandy, as they went into the store.

James nodded. "I hope she makes some of her chocolate cookies!"

The store was empty except for Mrs. Cox, who was sitting behind the counter reading a magazine. She was a tall, thin woman with an untidy bun of gray hair and round glasses.

"Hello, Martin," she said. "How are you? And how are the kittens and their mom?"

"They're fine, Mrs. Cox," said Martin.

"I'm glad to hear it," Mrs. Cox said. "What can I get for you and your friends?"

Martin gave her one of their posters. "We were wondering if you'd put this up in your window," he said.

Mrs. Cox unrolled the poster and looked at it. "Of course I will!" she said. "What a good idea! I'm sure lots of people in the village will come."

"We hope so," said Mandy.

The door opened, and Lucy came in. "Hello, Mrs. Cox," she said. Then she turned to Mandy, Martin, and James. "I've put all the posters up."

"So have we," said James.

"If you want to borrow any deck chairs, Lucy, I have some in my garden," Mrs. Cox offered. "And I can let you have some paper plates and plastic cups."

"Oh, thank you, Mrs. Cox!" said Lucy gratefully.

"Mrs. Ross is lending us some chairs and tables, too," said Mandy. "And she's going to bake some refreshments."

"Everyone's being so kind," said Lucy. "I hope the cats appreciate it!"

"Of course they will!" said Mandy.

"Martin and I will walk you two back to the hotel now," said Lucy, glancing at her watch. "Come on."

They said good-bye to Mrs. Cox and went out. Mandy was feeling cheerful again. As Lucy had pointed out, most people were being very helpful about the open house. Mandy was beginning to think that it couldn't possibly fail.

But there was a terrible shock waiting for them outside the store. Mr. Pengelly was standing there holding a clipboard. He was talking to a large man who wore a cap.

"... and this petition is to try to get that boatful of cats moved on," Mr. Pengelly was saying. He showed the man the papers he was holding. "As you can see, I've got some signatures already."

Mandy was upset. Mr. Pengelly hadn't wasted any time starting his petition. How many signatures did he have already? A lot or just a few? As they walked by, Mandy tried to sneak a look at the clipboard, but she couldn't see. Mr. Pengelly didn't notice them going by. He was too busy talking to the man in the cap.

"I'll sign it," Mandy heard the man say as they walked on. "My garbage can lid was knocked off again this morning, and there was trash all over my lawn. I'm fed up with it."

"It's not fair!" Mandy burst out as soon as they were out of earshot. "It could easily be a fox that's raiding the garbage cans!"

Lucy nodded. "Maybe we could ask if anyone in the village has seen foxes around at night."

"I wonder how many people have signed Mr. Pengelly's petition," James said anxiously.

Nobody answered, but everyone looked miserable. Then Mandy remembered the card she had made when they were designing the posters. She had slipped it into her pocket and forgotten about it. "Before we go to the hotel, may we go to Mr. Pengelly's house?" she asked Lucy.

"Mr. *Pengelly*'s house?" Martin and James said together, staring at Mandy in amazement. Lucy looked surprised, too.

Mandy took a deep breath. She was feeling unsure now, but it was too late to get out of it. She took the card she had made out of her pocket.

"I've made a special invitation for Mr. and Mrs. Pengelly," she explained. "I thought that maybe then they might come to the open house."

James looked doubtful. "I don't think they will."

Martin shook his head. "Me neither."

"Well, at least they can't say they haven't been invited!" Mandy said stubbornly.

"I think it's a very nice thought," Lucy agreed.

They walked to Mr. Pengelly's house. While the others waited at the gate, Mandy went up the walk and pushed the invitation through the mail slot. As she turned to leave, she noticed something very odd. There was a garbage can near the front door. The can was full, so the lid didn't fit tightly. Through the gap, Mandy

could see what looked like the edge of an empty cat food can.

Cat food? Mandy frowned. The Pengellys didn't have a cat. Why was there an empty cat food can in their garbage?

# 8

# *Helping Out*

"Well," said Dr. Adam as he turned the car down the road that led back to Bilbury, "I think we had a great time!"

"I did!" said Mandy eagerly. "The fox cubs were gorgeous!"

It was the following afternoon, and the Hopes and James had just returned from their visit to Roger Thomas, Dr. Adam's friend. They left after breakfast and drove to the wildlife hospital, a long bungalow with large grounds in the middle of the countryside.

As soon as Dr. Adam pulled up outside the building, Roger Thomas, a cheery-looking man with dark hair, came out to meet them.

"Adam! Emily!" he called. "Great to see you!" Roger welcomed Mandy and James, too. "I've heard you both like animals," he said with a twinkle in his eyes.

"We love animals!" said Mandy. She could hardly wait to see what kind of animals were being cared for at the hospital.

"Then you've come to the right place!" said Roger. "Come on, I'll give you the guided tour."

The hospital was looking after all sorts of sick wild animals. There was a young deer with a broken leg, two owls with injured wings, and several hedgehogs. There were also two fox cubs who had lost their mother.

Mandy smiled when she saw them. "They're

gorgeous!" she said softly, stroking their russet-colored heads.

"They're due to be fed soon," Roger told her. "You can help the nurse give them their milk if you like."

Mandy and James were thrilled. Roger gave each of them a cub to hold while the nurse got the bottles of milk. The cubs were full of energy and very curious. One of them even tried to go headfirst down James's sweatshirt. As soon as the milk arrived, the cubs settled down for their bottles.

"It's a bit like feeding a baby!" Mandy laughed as the cubs drained their bottles right down to the last drop.

After helping to feed the fox cubs, Mandy and James joined Roger and Dr. Adam and Dr. Emily for a delicious lunch before heading back to Bilbury.

Mandy had been so interested in the wildlife hospital and its patients, especially the fox cubs, that she had forgotten about *Puss-in-Boots* for a while. But now, as they drove into the village, she wondered what had happened while they were away. Had Mr. Pengelly been out collecting more signatures for his petition?

"Look!" said James suddenly. "Lucy and Martin!"

Lucy and Martin were walking up the main street carrying bags of groceries. Dr. Adam honked the horn and pulled over.

"Hello," called Dr. Emily, winding down the window. "How are you?"

"All right, thank you," said Lucy, although Mandy thought both she and Martin looked sad. "We were buying decorations and drinks for tomorrow."

"And we met Mr. Pengelly," Martin added. "You'll never guess what he's done!"

"What?" asked Mandy.

"He's called a meeting in the village hall on Monday night to discuss *Puss-in-Boots*!" Lucy said.

"Oh, no!" Mandy exclaimed.

"At least Mr. Pengelly's meeting is after the open house," James said. "Maybe by then we'll have enough people on our side."

"I hope so," Lucy sighed. Then she looked up at the sky and groaned. "Oh, no, it's starting to rain! That's all we need!"

Mandy's heart sank as big drops of rain began to splash onto the car's window. Who would want to come to the open house in weather like this?

"May we give you a lift?" asked Dr. Adam.

Lucy shook her head. "Thanks, but we've got more shopping to do."

"We'll see you tomorrow morning then," said Dr. Emily.

They waved good-bye to Lucy and Martin, and Dr. Adam drove on. Mandy gazed miserably up at the gray sky. The rain grew heavier. At this rate, it looked as if the open house was doomed.

# 9

# *Open House*

As soon as Mandy opened her eyes on Saturday morning, she jumped out of bed and hurried over to the window. She pulled the curtains back and looked outside. The sky was gray and overcast. Still, at least it wasn't raining, she thought.

The open house was scheduled to start at

two o'clock, and there was a lot of work to be done before then. After breakfast, Mandy and James helped Dr. Adam and Dr. Emily pack the car with deck chairs and tables. Mrs. Cox had given them a big silver urn to boil water for tea and coffee, as well as bags of plastic cups and cutlery and paper plates.

"At least that means there won't be any washing up to do when the open house is over!" Dr. Emily said, looking relieved.

At last everything was packed up, and Dr. Adam closed the doors. "We'll see you at *Puss-in-Boats*!" he called. He drove off with Dr. Emily. Mandy and James had promised to help Mrs. Ross pack up and deliver the cakes she had baked for the open house, so they hurried back into the hotel to find her.

"I can't wait for it to start," James said eagerly as they went toward the kitchen.

"Me, too." But Mandy couldn't help sounding a bit worried, and James frowned. "Are you all right, Mandy?" he asked.

Mandy nodded. "It's just — well, what if no one comes?"

"Of course people will come," James said. "No one would miss out on a great day like this!"

Mandy managed a smile. "I suppose not," she said. She knocked at the kitchen door.

"Come in," Mrs. Ross called.

Mandy and James opened the door and walked in. Their eyes grew wide with amazement. Lined up on the kitchen counter were four large, delicious-looking cakes, along with three plates piled high with cookies.

"Do you think that will be enough?" Mrs. Ross asked. "I didn't have time to make more."

"Mrs. Ross, it all looks great!" Mandy said, her eyes shining. Then she looked more closely at a plate of gingerbread cookies and began to laugh. "Oh, James, look!"

Instead of gingerbread men, Mrs. Ross had made gingerbread cats, with curly tails and raisins for eyes. Mandy and James were thrilled.

"I've had that cat-shaped cookie cutter for years and never used it," Mrs. Ross said, beaming at them. "I thought today was the *purr*-fect time to try it out!"

Mandy and James groaned at the joke. After they helped Mrs. Ross pack the cakes carefully into boxes, they set off to walk to *Puss-in-Boats*.

As they passed the poster they had put on the community board, Mandy wondered how many people had seen the posters and would decide to come. She wouldn't have to wait long to find out.

They turned down into the road where the Pengellys lived.

"I hope we don't meet Mr. Pengelly!" James whispered in Mandy's ear. But there was no one around except for a milkman. He was talking to a woman. It wasn't until they got closer that Mandy saw it was Mrs. Pengelly.

"And I'll have an extra bottle of milk, please," Mrs. Pengelly was saying.

The milkman smiled. "That makes three extra bottles this week!" he said. "Someone's drinking a lot of milk in your house!"

He handed three bottles to Mrs. Pengelly, who hurried back into the cottage.

"Do you know Mrs. Pengelly?" Mandy asked Mrs. Ross.

"Not very well," Mrs. Ross replied. "She keeps to herself. She doesn't say much."

"Mr. Pengelly doesn't give anyone a chance to say anything!" James pointed out.

Mrs. Ross smiled. "Well, let's hope he calms down and comes to the open house," she said.

They took the shortcut to the river across the fields. As they got closer to the barge, they could see that everyone was busy. Dr. Adam was setting out the tables and chairs on the riverbank, Dr. Emily and Lucy were standing on stepladders hanging streamers and balloons in the trees, and Martin was unpacking the plastic cups.

James went to help Martin, and Mrs. Ross

and Mandy began to set up the refreshments table.

"Mrs. Ross, you're marvelous!" Lucy exclaimed, as they unpacked the cakes and cookies. "Thank you so much for doing all this."

"It's a pleasure," said Mrs. Ross. "After all, you helped me when I needed it."

Mandy tried not to worry, but she couldn't help it. Would it rain? The sky still looked gray, although it was a little brighter than when she had woken up that morning. What if Mr. Pengelly had already turned most of the villagers against the barge?

Mandy hoped desperately that the day would be a success. She couldn't bear to think what would happen to *Puss-in-Boats'* cats if it wasn't.

It was almost two o'clock. The open house was about to start. Mandy stood on the riverbank looking around. The boat looked wonderful with its balloons and streamers and with Lucy's cat paintings displayed all over the cabin. There were balloons and streamers in the trees next to the boat, too. Some of the cats were lying on the deck, and some were strolling on the riverbank between the tables and chairs. Mandy looked for Queenie but couldn't see her.

Mrs. Ross was behind the refreshments table, which was crowded with the cakes and cookies that she and Lucy had baked. The hot water urn was steaming gently, ready for making tea and coffee, and pitchers of lemonade were lined up next to the piles of plastic cups. Everything was ready.

"I think we're all set!" Lucy smiled. She put her arm around Mandy's shoulders. "Now all we've got to do is wait for people to turn up!"

Mandy smiled back, even though her heart was pounding. Then, suddenly, James grabbed her arm.

"Look!" he said.

Mandy looked where James was pointing. A man, a woman, and a little girl were walking across the fields toward *Puss-in-Boats*. Her face lit up. "Are they coming here?"

"It looks like it," Dr. Adam said. "We'd better start stirring those pitchers of lemonade!"

An hour or so later, Mandy couldn't even remember why she'd been so worried. There had been just a few visitors at first, but then more and more started to arrive. Now the open house was in full swing.

Although the sky was still overcast, it hadn't rained, and now and then a gleam of pale sunshine broke through. There were people sitting around on the riverbank chatting, drinking tea and lemonade, and eating Mrs. Ross's and Lucy's cakes.

Some of the visitors were holding cats in their arms or on their laps. Mandy spotted Pusskin being petted by one man and Penny in the arms of a little girl. Meanwhile, Mandy's parents were busy answering questions about pet care, and especially about looking after cats. James and Martin had made a big sign reading ASK THE VET, and there was a long line of people waiting to speak to the Hopes.

Lucy was on the deck of *Puss-in-Boats*, and

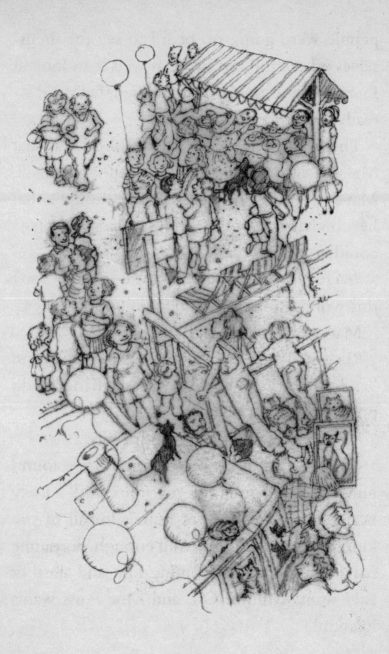

people were going on board to see for themselves where the cats lived, as well as to look at Lucy's paintings. Mandy could see that she'd already sold a few of them.

The only thing that wasn't so good was that Mr. and Mrs. Pengelly hadn't come, after all. Mandy sighed. She hadn't really thought that her invitation would do the trick, but she couldn't help hoping.

"Mandy!" Lucy hurried over to her. "Isn't this wonderful? Everything's going so well!"

Mandy grinned at her.

"I've sold four cat paintings," Lucy went on, "and two other people have asked me to do portraits of their pets."

"That's great!" Mandy said happily.

"But best of all, I think I might have found new homes for some of the cats!" Lucy beamed at her. "I've got homes for all of the kittens as soon as they're old enough. Someone has asked me about adopting Lily, and another lady wants Muffin. Oh, and Mrs. Ross wants Pusskin!"

That was the best news of all! To know that some of the cats would be going to loving homes was the best reward for all their hard work.

"Heavens!" Lucy said suddenly, sounding very surprised. "Here come Mr. and Mrs. Pengelly! I never expected to see them!"

Mandy's face lit up. Mr. and Mrs. Pengelly had come! Maybe her special invitation had done the trick after all. But when she looked over at the Pengellys, she wasn't so sure. Mr. Pengelly was marching along the riverbank with a large cardboard box in his arms, looking very red in the face. Mrs. Pengelly was hurrying along behind him, and she looked rather red, too.

Mandy felt her heart sink. The open house had been going so well. Had Mr. and Mrs. Pengelly come to spoil it?

# 10

# *A Confession*

Just at that moment, Mr. Pengelly spotted Lucy and Mandy. He headed straight toward them, looking very angry. Mrs. Pengelly scurried along behind him.

"Hello, Mr. Pengelly," Lucy said nervously. "We're so glad you decided to come."

"We're not here for the open house!"

snapped Mr. Pengelly. "We're here to return this!"

He pulled open the box he was holding, and Queenie stuck her head out. She saw Lucy and Mandy and began to meow loudly. Mandy bit her lip. It looked like the little cat had been caught in Mr. Pengelly's yard once again.

"Oh, Queenie!" Lucy sighed, lifting the cat out of the box. "Why can't you behave yourself?"

"I found her under my rosebush," Mr. Pengelly went on furiously. "And I want to know what you're going to do about it!"

Lucy looked helplessly at him. "I just don't know why Queenie keeps on going into your yard, Mr. Pengelly. I'm very sorry."

"That's not good enough!" snapped Mr. Pengelly. "And I'm not standing for it any longer!"

Mandy glanced at Mrs. Pengelly to see what she thought. But Mrs. Pengelly didn't look angry, she looked very embarrassed. Maybe she was just ashamed of Mr. Pengelly for making a scene at the open house. But maybe there was another reason.

Mandy remembered the empty can of cat food she had seen in the Pengellys' garbage can, as well as the extra bottles of milk Mrs. Pengelly had bought from the milkman.

"Excuse me, Mr. Pengelly," she said slowly. "I think I might know why Queenie keeps coming to your yard."

Mr. Pengelly stared at Mandy. "What do you mean?"

"Well," Mandy said, looking at Mrs. Pengelly, "cats keep going back to a place if someone there is feeding them."

Mrs. Pengelly turned bright red.

"No one's feeding that cat at *my* house!" Mr. Pengelly began crossly, but then his wife cleared her throat.

"Harry," she said quietly, "I think it's time for me to own up."

Mr. Pengelly turned to stare at his wife.

"I've been feeding Queenie," Mrs. Pengelly said.

*"You?"* spluttered Mr. Pengelly. "But why?"

Mrs. Pengelly smiled at her husband. "Because she reminds me of our Pepper," she said.

"Who's Pepper?" Mandy asked.

"The cat we had when we were first married," Mrs. Pengelly replied. She tickled Queenie under the chin. "You remember our Pepper, don't you, Harry?"

Mr. Pengelly stared hard at Queenie. "I suppose she does looks a bit like Pepper," he muttered reluctantly.

"Pepper was such a good cat!" Mrs. Pengelly went on. "Do you remember how he sat on your lap for hours in the evenings? He was so fond of you, Harry!"

Mr. Pengelly didn't say anything, but Mandy thought she saw him almost smile, even though he still looked embarrassed.

"We used to say that Pepper was the most handsome cat in town!" Mrs. Pengelly smiled at her husband. "Well, Queenie's just as beautiful."

Mrs. Pengelly put out her hand and gently

petted Queenie's head. The cat purred and climbed into her arms. "I'm sorry, Mrs. Browne." Mrs. Pengelly looked nervously at Lucy. "I thought Queenie was a stray when I started feeding her. I've been feeling very guilty about getting you into trouble."

"That's all right," Lucy said, and smiled at her. "I'm glad we've got this straightened out!"

Mandy looked at Mr. Pengelly. He didn't look angry anymore, just very embarrassed. Mandy couldn't help feeling a bit sorry for him.

"I'm sorry, Mrs. Browne," he muttered. "Obviously I didn't know that my wife was . . . er . . . encouraging the cat to come into our yard."

"Won't you both come and have some tea?" Lucy asked. "Then you can see how careful we are to look after the cats properly."

Mr. Pengelly shook his head. "I've got to get back home," he muttered. "Got some jobs to do in the yard."

"I'll stay for a little while," said Mrs. Pengelly. "I'd like a cup of tea. And then I'd like to have a look around *Puss-in-Boats*."

Mr. Pengelly hurried off. His wife went over to the refreshments table, still carrying Queenie in her arms.

Lucy turned to Mandy and patted her on the back. "How did you figure out that Mrs. Pengelly was feeding Queenie?"

Mandy explained about the extra milk Mrs. Pengelly was having delivered and the cat food can in the garbage. "But I didn't guess what they meant until I saw how embarrassed Mrs. Pengelly looked," she said.

"Well, let's hope that this will stop Mr. Pengelly from causing further trouble for *Puss-in-Boats*," Lucy said happily.

James and Martin came running over with Blackie at their heels. "What did Mr. Pengelly want?" asked James.

Lucy smiled at the two boys. "We'll tell you all about it," she said. "But first let's go over to the refreshments table, because Mandy deserves a big slice of chocolate cake!"

Mandy smiled. The open house was a success. Maybe now Mr. Pengelly would drop his petition against *Puss-in-Boats* and cancel the meeting at the village hall. Then Lucy and Martin and the cats would be able to stay. The day had been hard work, but it was worth it to keep the cats safe.

The open house was so popular, it continued into the early evening. When the last visitors left, the Hopes, James, Lucy, Martin, and Mrs. Ross started to clean up. They packed away the chairs and tables and picked up the trash. They didn't finish until very late.

"I think today has been the best part of the whole vacation!" James said with an enormous yawn.

"Well, I for one have never worked so hard on a vacation before!" Dr. Adam replied with a smile. "But it was definitely worth it."

"We've made a lot of money!" Lucy said happily. "I think we'll be able to start having the barge repaired very soon!"

Mandy was delighted. That meant that even if Lucy and Martin did have to move, at least they wouldn't have to leave the boat and the cats behind. If only Mr. Pengelly would stop his campaign to make *Puss-in-Boats* move, everything would be perfect. They would just have to wait and see what the man decided to do next.

"I can't believe we're going home today!" Mandy sighed. James and the Hopes and Blackie were walking along the riverbank. "I'm really going to miss *Puss-in-Boats*."

Dr. Emily put her arm around Mandy. "We all will," she said, "but at least we've done our very best to help."

Mandy nodded. It was Sunday morning, the day after the open house, and they were on their way to say good-bye to Lucy, Martin, and the cats before they went back home to Welford.

When they arrived at *Puss-in-Boats*, Martin was on deck feeding some of the cats. Lucy was down in the cabin, but she hurried out when they climbed aboard.

"Hello," Lucy called. "Are you ready to leave?"

"We'll be going in about an hour," said Dr. Emily.

"And how's Pusskin settling in at the hotel?" asked Lucy.

"He loves it," Mandy replied. "He and Mrs. Ross are great friends already."

Martin came over to them, carrying Queenie. "There's someone here who wants to say good-bye to you," he said, and he put the black cat into Mandy's arms.

"Hello, Queenie!" said Mandy, stroking the cat's head. "I'm going to miss you!"

"Me, too," said James. "After all, she was the one who brought us here."

"She's a very smart cat!" said Martin, tickling Queenie under the chin.

Mandy noticed a man coming across the fields toward the barge. She recognized him and frowned. "That's Mr. Pengelly!" she said.

Lucy looked nervous. "Oh, no!" she said. "What does he want now?"

They all waited in silence as Mr. Pengelly came up to the barge. Mandy's heart was beating quickly. Had Mr. Pengelly come to complain about something else?

Looking embarrassed, Mr. Pengelly nodded a good morning to everyone. Then he looked at Lucy. "I'd like a word with you, Mrs. Browne, if I may."

"Yes, of course," Lucy said. "Do come on board."

Mr. Pengelly climbed carefully onto the deck. "My wife and I had a long talk yesterday, and . . ." Mr. Pengelly stopped and cleared his throat. "She tells me that your boat is very clean and tidy." He glanced around the deck. "And I can see for myself that she's right."

Lucy smiled. "Thank you."

"I want you to know that I've called off my . . . er . . . campaign to make you and your cats move," Mr. Pengelly muttered. "I won't be going ahead with the petition or the meeting."

Mandy and James grinned at each other. *Puss-in-Boats* was safe!

"There's just one more thing." Mr. Pengelly looked even more embarrassed. "My wife's very upset at the thought of Queenie not coming around anymore." He looked at Queenie, who was still in Mandy's arms. "So I was wondering if we could . . . er . . . keep her."

Mandy could hardly believe her ears. "You mean you want to adopt her?"

Mr. Pengelly nodded. "If that's all right?" He looked at Lucy.

"Perfectly all right!" said Lucy cheerfully. "I think you and Mrs. Pengelly will give Queenie a wonderful home! We'll bring her over to you later on today, if you wish."

Mr. Pengelly nodded, turning even redder. He said a quick thank-you and good-bye, patted Queenie quickly on the head, and hurried away.

"Well!" said James, "Mrs. Ross said Mr. Pengelly wasn't a bad person, and she was right!"

"That's four cats who have found homes, as well as all the kittens," Mandy said.

"Five," said Martin. "The priest came to see us this morning. He wants to adopt Penny. He's got mice in the church!"

"I'm so glad we can stay!" Lucy said joyfully. "We've made some good friends here, and Martin will be able to go to the village school."

Mandy grinned. She could hardly believe how well things had turned out.

"Time for us to be going," said Dr. Adam, glancing at his watch.

"Good-bye, Queenie," said Mandy, and she gave the cat a final hug.

"Good-bye, Queenie," said James, doing the same. "We won't forget you!"

"And we won't forget *you!*" said Lucy.

"These are to say thank you for all your help!" She held up two small watercolor pictures of a black cat and gave one each to Mandy and James.

"It's Queenie!" James said. "Thanks!"

"Thank you very much!" Mandy added, her eyes shining with delight. The paintings would be the perfect reminder of a *purr*-fect summer vacation!